TEDD ARNOLD

HUGGLY
GETS DRESSED

SCHOLASTIC INC.

New York Toronto London Auckland Sydney

Look for Huggly in Scholastic's  **CD-ROM**

I'm Ready for Kindergarten

Huggly's Sleepover

Copyright © 1997 by Tedd Arnold.
All rights reserved. Published by Scholastic Inc.
HUGGLY and THE MONSTER UNDER THE BED are trademarks of Tedd Arnold. CARTWHEEL BOOKS and the CARTWHEEL BOOKS logo are trademarks and/or registered trademarks of Scholastic Inc.

Library of Congress Cataloging-in-Publication Data
Arnold, Tedd.
   Huggly gets dressed / by Tedd Arnold.
      p.   cm. — (Monsters under the bed)
   "Cartwheel books."
   Summary: A monster from under the bed tries to wear people clothes.
   ISBN 0-590-11759-9
   [1. Monsters — Fiction.   2. Clothing and dress — Fiction.]
I. Title.   II. Series.
PZ7.A7379Hu   1997
[E] — dc21   97-18777
                                                                        CIP
                                                                         AC
10   01 02

Printed in the U.S.A.   24
First printing, December 1997

Huggly peeked out from under the bed.

It was dark and quiet in the room. And messy. Perfect! He didn't want to wake the people child on the bed.

He hopped across the room on tippy-toes.
On tippy-top. On tippy-tail.

He bumped his head.

Things fell onto the floor. It was the stuff people wear on their bodies.

He wondered why they wear the stuff.
He wondered how.
Huggly decided to try for himself.

A bright red-and-yellow striped thing had a nice hole for his tail.

He slipped his arms into a blue thing.

He found a pair of orange things for his toes.

He pulled long purple things over his hands.

A white thing fit snugly on his head.

There was a green thing that he just couldn't figure out.

Huggly said to himself, "So this is how people dress!" There was a knock on the door. "Time to wake up, Sleepyhead," the people mother said. "Do you need help getting dressed?"

Huggly froze with fear. What if the people caught him? "Oh no!" he said out loud before he could stop himself.

"Did you say no?" the mother asked. "Are you sure?"
She turned the knob to open the door.

Huggly had to act quickly. Pulling things off his arms and legs, he turned and ran...

bump...right into Sleepyhead.

ust as the door swung open, Huggly dived under the bed.

"Silly, Sleepyhead." The mother laughed.
"How did you get dressed like that?"

"A...a...monster under the bed...," Sleepyhead mumbled.
"That goofy monster again?" his mother said.
"Tell me all about it."

THE HOUND OF THE
BASKERVILLES

THE HOUND OF THE BASKERVILLES

ADAPTED FROM THE ORIGINAL NOVEL BY
SIR ARTHUR CONAN DOYLE
ILLUSTRATED BY
I.N.J. CULBARD
TEXT ADAPTED BY
IAN EDGINTON

STERLING

New York / London
www.sterlingpublishing.com

Published by Sterling Publishing Co., Inc.
387 Park Avenue South, New York, NY 10016

Copyright © 2009 SelfMadeHero

First published 2009
by SelfMadeHero
A division of Metro Media Ltd
5 Upper Wimpole Street
London W1G 6BP
www.selfmadehero.com

Illustrator: I.N.J. Culbard
Adaptor: Ian Edginton
Cover Designers: I.N.J. Culbard and Jeff Willis
Designer: Andy Huckle
Publishing Director: Emma Hayley
With thanks to: Doug Wallace, Jane Laporte and Nick de Somogyi

Dedications
For Katy and Joseph for their love and patience.
For my mother for believing in me from the very beginning.
For my dear friend Colin, for all his help and without whom...
– I. N. J. Culbard

To the trio of lovely ladies in my life: my wife, Jane, and
daughters, Constance and Corinthia – Ian Edginton

Distributed in Canada by Sterling Publishing
c/o Canadian Manda Group, 165 Dufferin Street,
Toronto, Ontario, Canada M6K 3H6

Printed and bound in China

ISBN: 978-1-4027-7000-5

10 9 8 7 6 5 4 3 2 1

For information about custom editions, special sales, premium
and corporate purchases, please contact Sterling Special Sales
Department at 800-805-5489 or specialsales@sterlingpub.com.

FOREWORD

THE FOOTPRINTS OF A GIGANTIC HOUND...

Sherlock Holmes wasn't supposed to be in this book.

When Conan Doyle set to work in March of 1901, he simply wanted to write what he called "a real creeper." In a note to his mother he proposed a title, *The Hound of the Baskervilles*, but there was no mention of his famous detective. As the novel progressed, however, Conan Doyle found that he needed a strong central figure to hold the plot together. "Why should I invent such a character," he said, "when I have him already in the form of Holmes?"

There was one problem: Sherlock Holmes was supposed to be dead. Eight years earlier, in a story called "The Final Problem," Holmes had been dragged to his death by the notorious Professor Moriarty at Switzerland's Reichenbach Falls. "I have been much blamed for doing that gentleman to death," wrote the weary author, "but I hold that it was not murder, but justifiable homicide in self-defense, since, if I had not killed him, he would certainly have killed me."

Now, however, as *The Hound of the Baskervilles* took shape, Conan Doyle relented and brought the detective back for a curtain call. "I have nearly finished 'Sherlock,'" he told his mother as the manuscript neared completion, "and I hope he will live up to his reputation."

He needn't have worried. On the morning of publication in *The Strand* magazine, home of the original Holmes tales, a long line of expectant readers stood waiting for copies, and bribes were offered for advance peeks. The subsequent book edition became a massive bestseller, and would go on to become one of the most popular novels of the 20th century.

Not surprisingly, this success brought pressure for more Sherlock Holmes stories. Conan Doyle had made it clear that *The Hound* was nothing more than a previously untold tale, predating the fatal encounter with Professor Moriarty. Soon, however, the American magazine *Collier's Weekly* offered a staggering sum of money for a series of new adventures featuring a fully resurrected Holmes. Bowing to the inevitable, Conan Doyle signalled his acceptance with a laconic postcard: "Very well. A.C.D." All that remained was to figure out how the detective had survived his apparent death at the Reichenbach Falls.

But that's a different story...

— Daniel Stashower
author of the Edgar Award-winning
Teller of Tales: The Life of Arthur Conan Doyle

NOT THAT YOU ARE ENTIRELY WRONG IN THIS INSTANCE. THE MAN CERTAINLY IS A COUNTRY PRACTITIONER. HOWEVER, SUCH A PRESENTATION TO A DOCTOR IS MORE LIKELY TO COME FROM A HOSPITAL THAN A HUNT.

THE INITIALS "C.C.": THE WORDS "CHARING CROSS" VERY NATURALLY SUGGEST THEMSELVES!

WHEN DR. MORTIMER WITHDREW FROM THE HOSPITAL TO START A PRACTICE FOR HIMSELF, HIS FRIENDS UNITED TO GIVE HIM THIS PLEDGE OF THEIR GOODWILL.

HE WAS ONLY A HOUSE SURGEON OR PHYSICIAN, SINCE ONLY A MAN WELL ESTABLISHED IN A LONDON PRACTICE WOULD BE ON THE HOSPITAL STAFF AND NO SUCH PHYSICIAN WOULD DRIFT INTO THE COUNTRY.

HE LEFT FIVE YEARS AGO, OBSERVE, THE DATE IS ON THE STICK!

SO YOUR GRAVE FAMILY PRACTITIONER VANISHES INTO THIN AIR, MY DEAR WATSON, AND EMERGES A YOUNG FELLOW UNDER THIRTY. AMIABLE, UNAMBITIOUS, ABSENT-MINDED AND THE POSSESSOR OF A FAVORITE DOG!

I SHOULD DESCRIBE IT AS BEING LARGER THAN A TERRIER, BUT SMALLER THAN A MASTIFF.

I'VE NO MEANS OF CHECKING THAT, BUT I DO KNOW HOW TO FIND OUT A FEW PARTICULARS OF THE MAN'S AGE AND CAREER — THE MEDICAL DIRECTORY!

THE CURSE OF THE BASKERVILLES

THIS FAMILY PAPER WAS COMMITTED TO MY CARE BY SIR CHARLES BASKERVILLE, WHO DIED IN SUDDEN AND TRAGIC CIRCUMSTANCES THREE MONTHS AGO.

I MAY SAY THAT I WAS HIS PERSONAL FRIEND AS WELL AS HIS PHYSICIAN.

HE WAS A STRONG-MINDED MAN. SHREWD, PRACTICAL AND AS UNIMAGINATIVE AS I AM MYSELF.

YET--- HE TOOK THIS DOCUMENT VERY SERIOUSLY AND HIS MIND WAS PREPARED FOR JUST SUCH AN END AS DID EVENTUALLY OVERTAKE HIM.

IT APPEARS TO BE A STATEMENT OF SOME SORT... DATED 1742? I UNDERSTOOD IT WAS A MORE MODERN AND PRACTICAL MATTER UPON WHICH YOU WISHED TO CONSULT ME?

MOST MODERN, BUT THE MANUSCRIPT CONCERNING A CERTAIN LEGEND WHICH RUNS IN THE BASKERVILLE FAMILY IS INTIMATELY CONNECTED WITH THE AFFAIR.

"THEY PASSED A NIGHT SHEPHERD UPON THE MOOR AND DEMANDED TO KNOW IF HE HAD SEEN THE HUNT."

"CRAZED WITH FEAR, HE SAID HE HAD SEEN THE MAIDEN WITH THE HOUNDS ON HER TRACK, HUGO BASKERVILLE ON HIS BLACK MARE, AND RUNNING MUTE BEHIND HIM A HOUND OF HELL AT HIS HEELS!"

"CURSING THE SHEPHERD, THE DRUNKEN SQUIRES RODE ON, BUT THEIR SKINS TURNED COLD AS THE BLACK MARE WENT PAST, TRAILING ITS BRIDLE AND EMPTY SADDLE."

"RIDING SLOWLY, THEY CAME UPON THE HOUNDS, WHIMPERING IN A CLUSTER, STARING EYES GAZING DOWN THE NARROW VALLEY BEFORE THEM."

"MORE SOBER THAN WHEN THEY STARTED, THREE OF THE BOLDEST RODE FORWARD INTO THE DEEP DIP OR GOYAL."

THE FACTS OF THE CASE ARE SIMPLE. BEFORE GOING TO BED, SIR CHARLES WAS IN THE HABIT OF TAKING A NOCTURNAL WALK DOWN BASKERVILLE HALL'S FAMOUS YEW ALLEY.

HE WAS TO START FOR LONDON THE NEXT DAY AND ORDERED BARRYMORE TO PREPARE HIS LUGGAGE.

AT MIDNIGHT, BARRYMORE, FINDING THE HALL DOOR STILL OPEN, BECAME ALARMED AND WENT IN SEARCH OF HIS MASTER.

THE DAY HAD BEEN WET AND SIR CHARLES' FOOTPRINTS WERE EASILY TRACED DOWN THE ALLEY. HALFWAY ALONG IS A GATE THAT LEADS OUT ONTO THE MOOR.

SIR CHARLES HAD EVIDENTLY STOOD THERE FOR SOME TIME BEFORE PROCEEDING DOWN TO THE FAR END OF THE ALLEY WHERE HIS BODY WAS DISCOVERED.

"HE HAD TAKEN THE LEGEND TO HEART AND WAS HONESTLY CONVINCED THAT A DREADFUL FATE OVERHUNG HIS FAMILY."

"I REMEMBER, VISITING SOME THREE WEEKS BEFORE THE FATAL EVENT, I HAD DESCENDED FROM MY GIG WHEN I SAW HIS EYES STARE PAST ME WITH AN EXPRESSION OF THE MOST DREADFUL HORROR!"

"I TURNED IN TIME TO GLIMPSE WHAT I TOOK TO BE A LARGE, BLACK CALF PASSING THE HEAD OF THE DRIVE. HOWEVER, THE INCIDENT MADE THE WORST IMPRESSION UPON HIS MIND."

"HIS HEART, TOO, I KNEW WAS AFFECTED BY THE CONSTANT ANXIETY. IT WAS ON MY ADVICE THAT HE WAS ABOUT TO GO TO LONDON AND ENJOY THE DISTRACTIONS OF THE TOWN. MR. STAPLETON, A MUTUAL FRIEND, WAS OF THE SAME OPINION."

THEN CAME THE NIGHT OF THIS TERRIBLE CATASTROPHE. BARRYMORE HAD SENT PERKINS THE GROOM TO FETCH ME...

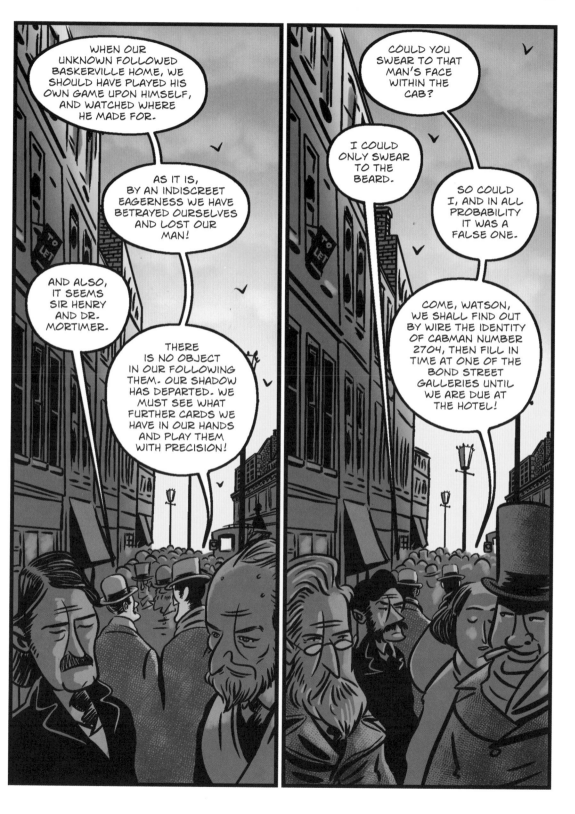

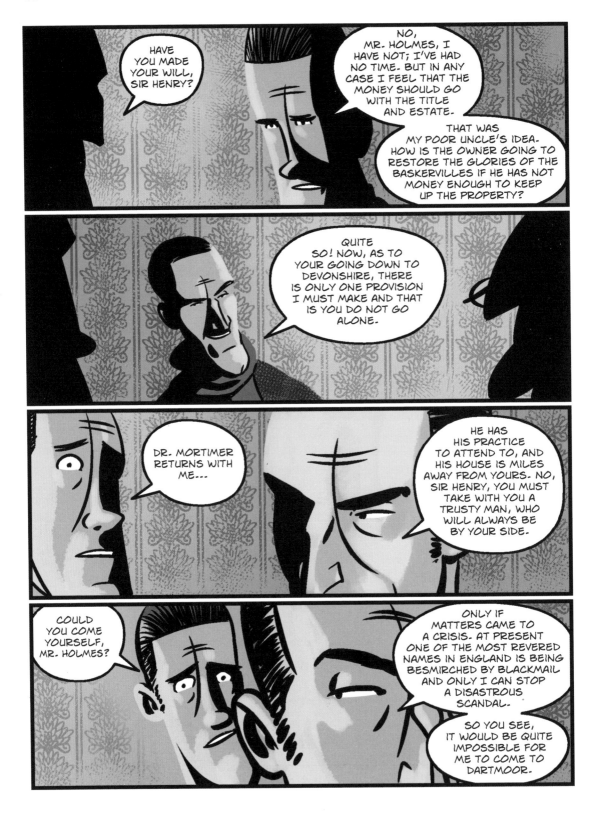

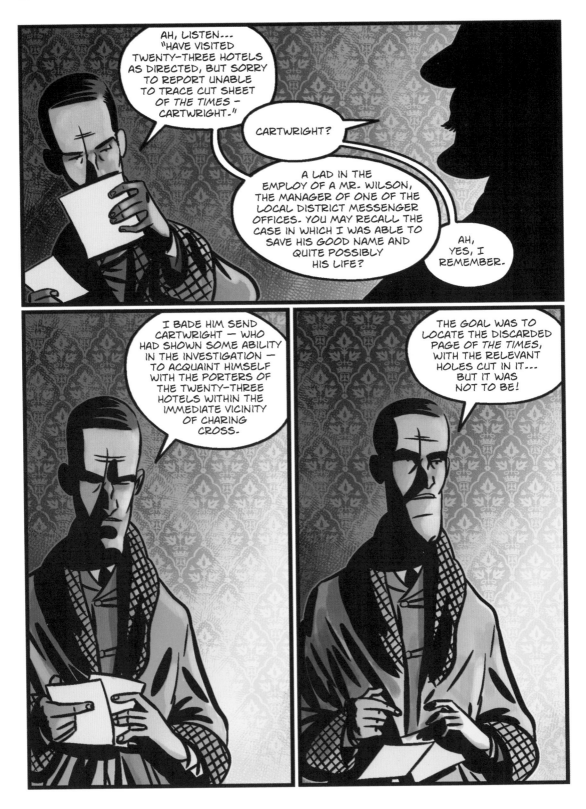

FIRST REPORT OF DR. WATSON

Baskerville Hall, Oct. 13.

My Dear Holmes,

The longer one stays here in this God-forsaken corner of the world, the more does the spirit of the moor sink into one's soul.

But I digress....

SEVERAL INCIDENTS HAVE OCCURRED OF LATE, NOT LEAST OF WHICH IS THE BELIEF THAT THE MURDERER, SELDEN, HAS GOT AWAY.

A FORTNIGHT HAS PASSED SINCE HIS FLIGHT, DURING WHICH HE HAS NOT BEEN SEEN NOR HEARD OF.

IT IS INCONCEIVABLE THAT HE HELD OUT UPON THE MOOR ALL THAT TIME. WE THINK THEREFORE THAT HE HAS GONE.

HE IS AN ELDERLY, RED-FACED GENTLEMAN, WITH A PASSION FOR BRITISH LAW, AND HAS SPENT A LARGE FORTUNE IN LITIGATION.

THIS ASIDE, HE SEEMS A KINDLY AND GOOD-NATURED PERSON.

HE'S AN AMATEUR ASTRONOMER AND OWNS AN EXCELLENT TELESCOPE WITH WHICH HE SWEEPS THE MOOR IN THE HOPE OF CATCHING A GLIMPSE OF THE ESCAPED CONVICT!

HOWEVER, AS I CLOSE, LET ME TELL YOU MORE ABOUT THE BARRYMORES AND LAST NIGHT'S SURPRISING DEVELOPMENTS.

MRS. BARRYMORE IS A HEAVY, SOLID PERSON, VERY LIMITED, INTENSELY RESPECTABLE AND INCLINED TO BE PURITANICAL. YOU COULD HARDLY CONCEIVE A LESS EMOTIONAL SUBJECT.

BARRYMORE WAS CROUCHING AT A WINDOW, STARING OUT AT THE BLACKNESS OF THE MOOR. FOR SOME MINUTES HE STOOD, WATCHING INTENTLY.

THEN HE GAVE A DEEP GROAN AND WITH AN IMPATIENT GESTURE HE PUT OUT THE LIGHT.

THERE IS SOME SECRET BUSINESS GOING ON HERE IN THIS HOUSE OF GLOOM.

I HAVE SPOKEN TO SIR HENRY THIS MORNING, AND WE HAVE MADE A PLAN OF CAMPAIGN, FOUNDED UPON MY OBSERVATIONS. I WILL NOT SPEAK OF IT NOW, BUT IT SHOULD MAKE MY NEXT REPORT INTERESTING READING.

THE LIGHT UPON THE MOOR (SECOND REPORT OF DR. WATSON)

Baskerville Hall, Oct. 15

My Dear Holmes,
If I was compelled to leave you without much news during the first days of my mission, I am clearly making up for lost time as events are crowding thick and fast upon us.

SIR HENRY MEANS TO SPARE NO EXPENSE IN RESTORING THE GRANDEUR OF HIS FAMILY.

THERE HAVE BEEN DECORATORS AND FURNISHERS UP FROM PLYMOUTH AND A CONTRACTOR FROM LONDON.

WITH THE HOUSE REFURBISHED, ALL HE WILL NEED IS A WIFE TO MAKE IT COMPLETE — AND, BETWEEN OURSELVES, THERE ARE SIGNS THIS WILL NOT BE WANTING IF THE LADY IS WILLING.

EXTRACT FROM THE DIARY OF DR. WATSON

OCTOBER 16
I AM CONSCIOUS OF A FEELING OF IMPENDING DANGER WHICH IS MORE TERRIBLE BECAUSE I AM UNABLE TO DEFINE IT.

THE FIGURE ON THE TOR IS NO ONE I HAVE SEEN DOWN HERE, I AM CERTAIN. A STRANGER, THEN, IS DOGGING US, JUST AS IN LONDON.

MY FIRST IMPULSE WAS TO TELL SIR HENRY, BUT HIS NERVES HAVE BEEN STRANGELY SHAKEN BY THAT SOUND UPON THE MOOR.

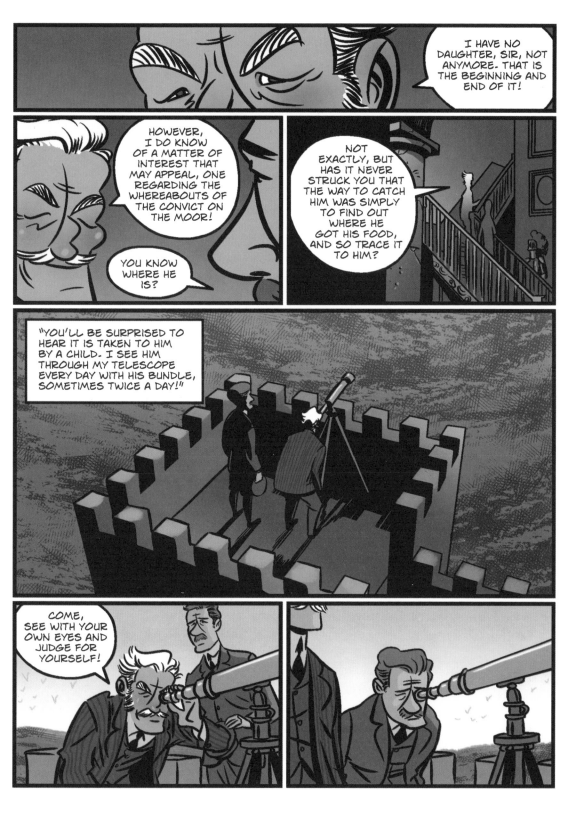

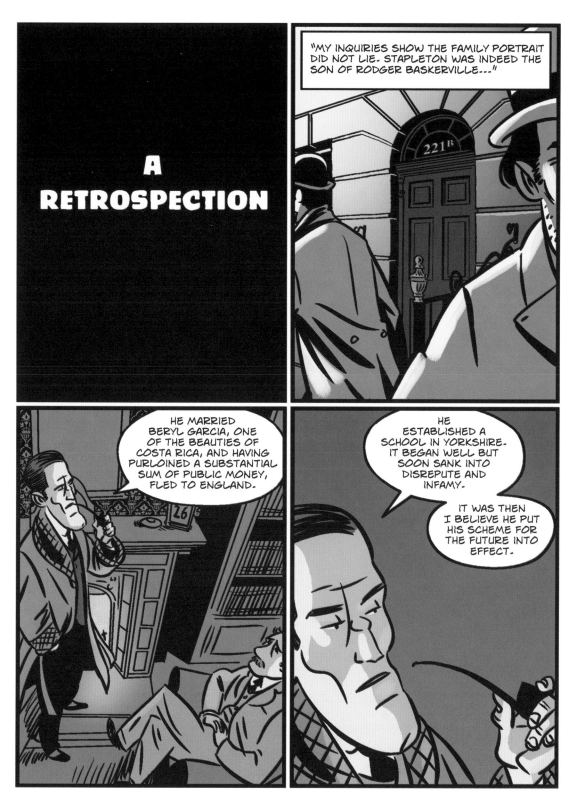

SKETCHBOOK...

WITH NOTES BY THE ILLUSTRATOR,
I. N. J. CULBARD

WITH BOTH THESE EARLY JACKET COVER DESIGNS I WANTED TO CAPTURE THE PULP ADVENTURE FEEL TO THE SHERLOCK HOLMES STORIES SO I WENT FOR AGED-LOOKING CREASED COVERS. HERE (RIGHT) WE HAVE A ROUGH EARLY DESIGN OF HOLMES AND WATSON SET AGAINST THE BLEAK BACKDROP OF THE MOOR, AND THE HOUND FRAMED BY MOONLIGHT ON THE TOR. I BASED THE HOUND'S SILHOUETTE ON THE IMAGE OF THE HOUND WHICH APPEARED ON THE COVER OF THE BOOK'S FIRST EDITION.

HERE'S A JACKET DESIGN PRODUCED LATER ON ONCE I'D ESTABLISHED HOLMES' APPEARANCE, BUT AS YOU MAY SEE FROM THIS PICTURE I WAS STILL TRYING TO FIGURE OUT WHAT MY VERSION OF WATSON WOULD LOOK LIKE.

HOLMES IS IN HIS MID-THIRTIES WHEN *THE HOUND OF THE BASKERVILLES* TAKES PLACE. THE DESCRIPTION OF HIM GIVEN BY DR. WATSON IN *A STUDY IN SCARLET* PROVIDED ME WITH A FEW POINTERS. HIS EYES WERE "SHARP AND PIERCING" AND HIS NOSE "THIN" AND "HAWK-LIKE," WITH A CHIN THAT HAD "THE PROMINENCE OF SQUARENESS WHICH MARK THE MAN OF DETERMINATION." THESE ARE JUST SOME EARLY DESIGNS.

WATSON IS DESCRIBED AS THICK-SET AND SQUARE-JAWED. AFTER SEVERAL ATTEMPTS (SEEN ON THIS PAGE) I CONCLUDED THAT WATSON'S APPEARANCE OUGHT TO COMPLEMENT HOLMES' BY BEING QUITE CONTRARY. SO WHILE HOLMES' HAIR WAS SLICK AND STRAIGHT, IT SEEMED SENSIBLE TO HAVE WATSON'S BE THICKER AND WAVY. HOLMES' NOSE IS ANGULAR WITH A PROMINENT BRIDGE, SO WATSON'S IS FLAT ACROSS THE BRIDGE AND SMOOTH, AND SO ON...

THE ROOMS AT 221B BAKER STREET

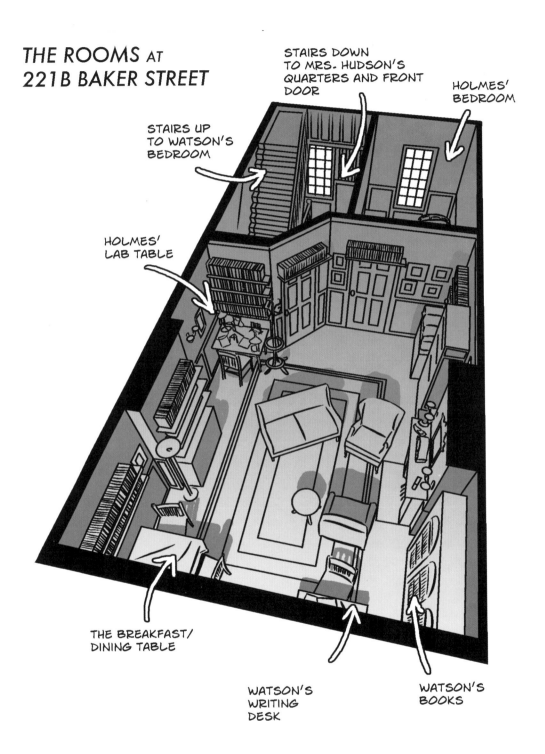

STAIRS DOWN TO MRS. HUDSON'S QUARTERS AND FRONT DOOR

HOLMES' BEDROOM

STAIRS UP TO WATSON'S BEDROOM

HOLMES' LAB TABLE

THE BREAKFAST/ DINING TABLE

WATSON'S WRITING DESK

WATSON'S BOOKS

COMING SOON...

A STUDY
IN SCARLET

A *STUDY IN SCARLET* IS WHERE IT ALL BEGAN: THE ORIGINAL
STORY OF THE FIRST EVER "CONSULTING DETECTIVE,"
MR. SHERLOCK HOLMES OF BAKER STREET, AND HIS NEW
HOUSEMATE, THEN FRIEND, NOW IMMORTAL CHRONICLER,
DR. JOHN WATSON. FIRST PUBLISHED AS THE "REPRINT" OF
WATSON'S "REMINISCENCES" IN 1887, SIR ARTHUR CONAN
DOYLE'S NOVEL HAS SET THE STANDARD OF FORENSIC
DEDUCTION FOR EVERY WHODUNNIT SINCE. THE TITLE OF
A *STUDY IN SCARLET* DELIBERATELY SUGGESTS THE SEMI-
ABSTRACT PAINTINGS THEN BECOMING FASHIONABLE –
BUT THE ART IT PIONEERED HAS LASTED MUCH LONGER.
AS HOLMES HIMSELF PUTS IT, "THERE'S THE SCARLET THREAD
OF MURDER RUNNING THROUGH THE COLORLESS SKEIN OF LIFE,
AND OUR DUTY IS TO UNRAVEL IT, AND ISOLATE IT,
AND EXPOSE EVERY INCH OF IT."

PREVIEW...

MR. SHERLOCK HOLMES

IN THE YEAR 1878, I TOOK MY DEGREE AS DOCTOR OF MEDICINE AT THE UNIVERSITY OF LONDON BEFORE PROCEEDING TO NETLEY AND THE COURSE PRESCRIBED FOR ARMY SURGEONS. UPON COMPLETING MY STUDIES, I WAS ATTACHED TO THE FIFTH NORTHUMBERLAND FUSILIERS AS ASSISTANT SURGEON.

BEFORE I COULD JOIN THE REGIMENT IN INDIA, THE SECOND AFGHAN WAR HAD BROKEN OUT. MY CORPS WERE DEEP IN THE ENEMY'S COUNTRY. I EVENTUALLY REACHED THEM IN CANDAHAR AND AT ONCE ENTERED UPON MY NEW DUTIES.

THE CAMPAIGN BROUGHT HONORS AND PROMOTION TO MANY, BUT FOR ME IT HELD NOTHING BUT MISFORTUNE AND DISASTER.

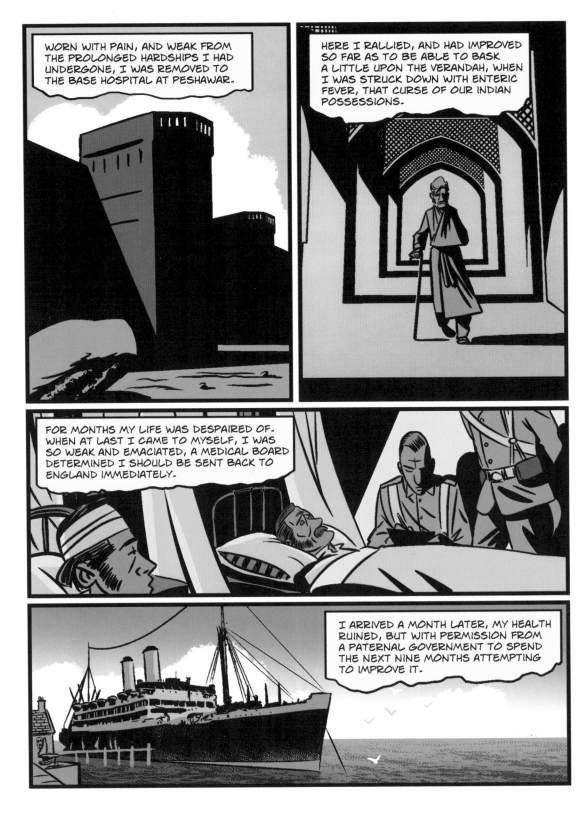